Finding Out About THINGS THAT GO

Written by: **Eliot Humberstone**

Designed by: **Iain Ashman**

Consultant Editor: **Betty Root**

Science Consultants: **Anthony Wilson** **Aubrey Tulley**

Researcher: **Nigel Flynn**

Illustrated by:

Basil Arm
Louise Nevett
Eric Smart
Graham Smith
Clive Spong
Mike Roffe
Gordon Wylie

Contents

Ferry boats

The boat in this picture is a ferry. It can carry lots of passengers, cars and lorries. They drive on at the front and drive off at the back.

This is the funnel. Waste gas from the ship's diesel engines comes out here.

The small boats on the top deck are life boats. They can be lowered over the side if the ship starts to sink.

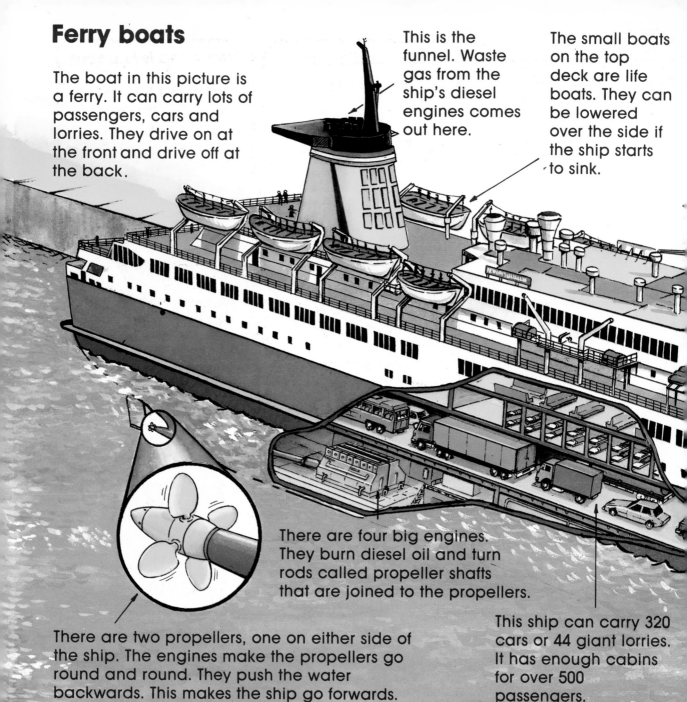

There are four big engines. They burn diesel oil and turn rods called propeller shafts that are joined to the propellers.

There are two propellers, one on either side of the ship. The engines make the propellers go round and round. They push the water backwards. This makes the ship go forwards.

This ship can carry 320 cars or 44 giant lorries. It has enough cabins for over 500 passengers.

2

These are radar scanners. They send out radio signals. These signals bounce off ships or land nearby. This helps the captain when it is dark or foggy. Radar helps to stop accidents.

Loading the ferry

The bow of the ship, which is the front, is hinged. When the ship is in port, the bow lifts up so cars and lorries can drive on.

How deep is the sea?

To find out how deep the sea is, modern ships use an echo sounder. This sends a sound down to the sea-bed.

Signal from ship

Echo returning to ship

The sound echoes back to the ship. The depth of water is worked out from the time it takes the echo to come back to the ship.

When cars and lorries go on and off the ship, they drive over the drawbridge. This lifts up when the ship leaves port.

3

Sailing boats

These small sailing boats are called dinghies. If you sail in a dinghy you need to keep close to the coast as it is not safe to go out in rough seas.

The sail of a boat is made of light nylon material. By moving the boom, the sail can be turned around so it catches the wind. The wind pushes the boat along.

This is called a boom. It can swing round to either side of the boat. This helps the sail to catch the wind.

Steering the boat

The tiller is for steering the boat. It is fixed to the rudder. When you pull the tiller one way, it pushes the rudder in the opposite direction.

Water pushing against the rudder helps turn the boat around.

The centre board is below the boat. It is a flat board that goes into the water. This stops the wind blowing the boat along sideways.

4

In the past

In the past, large sailing ships used to carry goods and passengers all around the world. Some were 100 metres long and some had as many as five masts. They needed a crew of up to 50 people to work all the sails.

Catamarans and trimarans

Most boats have only one hull. It is smooth and pointed to go through the water easily.

Hull

Catamaran

Trimaran

Some boats, called catamarans, have two hulls. Others, called trimarans, have three hulls. These boats are faster than ordinary boats of the same size and they do not tip over very easily.

5

Submarines

Submarines have large tanks called ballast tanks. These can be filled with water or air to make the submarine go down or up.

To go down, the ballast tanks are filled with water. This makes the submarine heavy, so it sinks.

In order to stay at the same depth, the water in the tanks is moved around to different tanks, to keep the submarine steady.

To come up, the ballast tanks are filled with air. This makes the submarine light so it rises.

Ballast tank

This small submarine is called a submersible. It is used for repairing oil rigs and for checking cables on the sea-bed. The submersible is put on a boat and taken out to sea. Then it is lowered over the side.

This is a mechanical arm. It can pick things up from the sea-bed.

The ballast tanks are in here.

Two little motors at the front steer the submersible.

Bright spotlights are needed to light up the dark sea-bed.

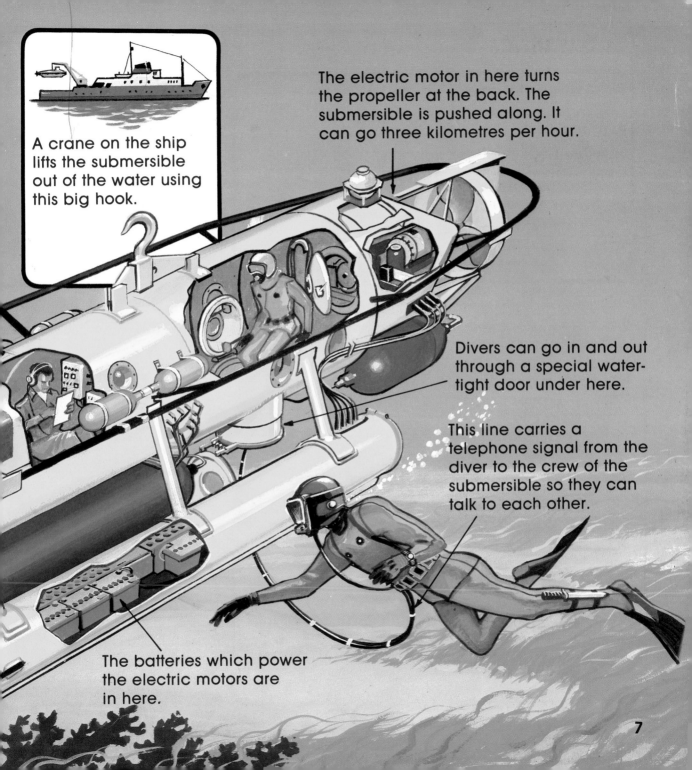

A crane on the ship lifts the submersible out of the water using this big hook.

The electric motor in here turns the propeller at the back. The submersible is pushed along. It can go three kilometres per hour.

Divers can go in and out through a special water-tight door under here.

This line carries a telephone signal from the diver to the crew of the submersible so they can talk to each other.

The batteries which power the electric motors are in here.

Hydrofoils

A hydrofoil is a boat that can move on the top of the water. It is raised up on metal wings called foils. It goes much faster than an ordinary boat because most of its body presses against air, not against water.

The foils can be lifted and lowered on these legs

When it is moving slowly, a hydrofoil floats on the water like an ordinary boat. As it goes faster, the foils are lowered into the water. Water going over the foils pushes them up and so the boat rises.

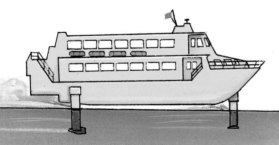

When it is going very fast, most of the hull is out of the water. Only the foils are in the water. The engine is above the middle of the back foil.

This hydrofoil can carry up to 245 passengers. Hydrofoils are used for going across short pieces of sea. They can go twice as fast as ordinary ferries.

Engine

Water shoots out here

The engine in this hydrofoil sucks in water, turns it round and round, and then shoots it out the back. This pushes the boat along.

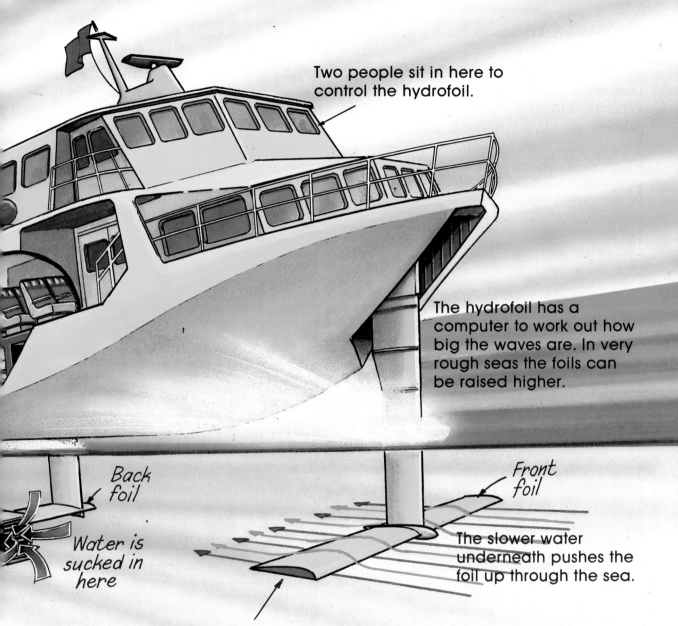

Two people sit in here to control the hydrofoil.

The hydrofoil has a computer to work out how big the waves are. In very rough seas the foils can be raised higher.

Back foil

Water is sucked in here

Front foil

The slower water underneath pushes the foil up through the sea.

The foil is flat on the bottom and curved on top, like an aeroplane wing. Water going over the top of the foil has to go faster than the water going below. Water going past the foil lifts it up in the same way that moving air keeps an aeroplane flying.

How planes fly

The aeroplane on these pages is a small two-seater plane. It is the kind of plane you learn to fly in.

This is one of the elevators. If the pilot turns them up, the plane goes up. If the pilot turns them down, the plane goes down.

The rudder is for steering the plane. When air rushes against the rudder, it turns the plane the way the rudder is pointing.

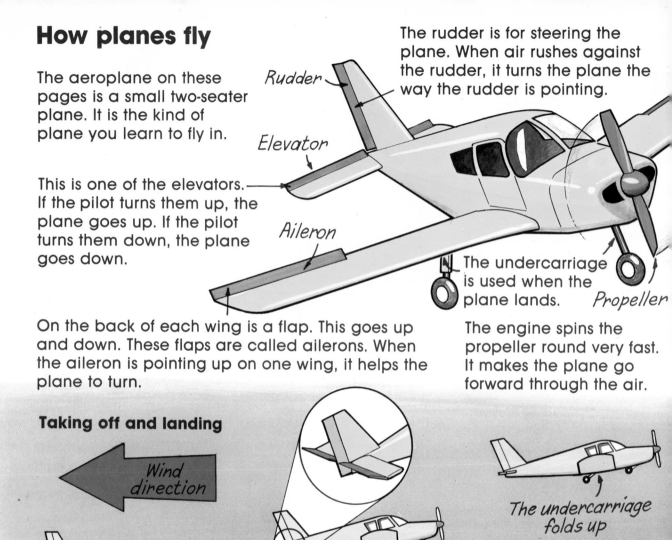

Rudder

Elevator

Aileron

The undercarriage is used when the plane lands.

Propeller

On the back of each wing is a flap. This goes up and down. These flaps are called ailerons. When the aileron is pointing up on one wing, it helps the plane to turn.

The engine spins the propeller round very fast. It makes the plane go forward through the air.

Taking off and landing

Wind direction

Elevators raised

The undercarriage folds up

Before they can take off, planes must go fast along the ground. This makes the air rush past their wings.

To make the plane climb, the pilot must raise the elevator flaps at the back of the plane. This helps the air underneath the wings push up on them so the plane is supported in the air.

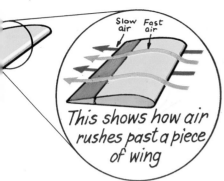

This shows how air rushes past a piece of wing

Wings are usually flat underneath and curved on top. This makes air go faster over the top, so there is less air there. The wings are pushed up by air from below trying to fill the space above them.

How wings work

Blow over the top of the paper

The best way to see how an aeroplane wing works is to try this test. Blow hard just above a sheet of paper. Your breath is like the fast air above a wing. There is less air on top, so the paper is lifted up by the air below.

Elevators lowered

Elevators are lifted slightly just before landing

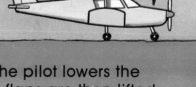

The pilot turns off the engine when the plane has landed

To come down, the pilot lowers the elevators. Air pushes against them and the plane goes down.

As the plane comes down, the pilot lowers the undercarriage. The elevator flaps are then lifted slightly. This raises the plane so that the wheels touch down first.

Jumbo jets

The last two pages showed you how all planes fly. Jet airliners are large planes. Many people can fly in them. They can go a long way.

The cockpit is right in the front of the plane. The pilot, the co-pilot and the flight engineer sit there.

Some Jumbos can carry over 400 passengers. During the flight, they can watch films.

Jumbo jets are the biggest passenger planes in the world. People can go up a spiral staircase to the top deck.

There are four engines on a Jumbo jet, two under each wing.

How the engine works

A jet engine takes in air at the front and pushes it very fast through the back. When the air is forced out through the back, the plane is pushed forwards.

The fan spins round very fast and takes in air from the front. It shoots the air out very fast at the back.

Fuel like petrol mixes with air and burns in here. Hot gases shoot out at the back and push the plane forwards.

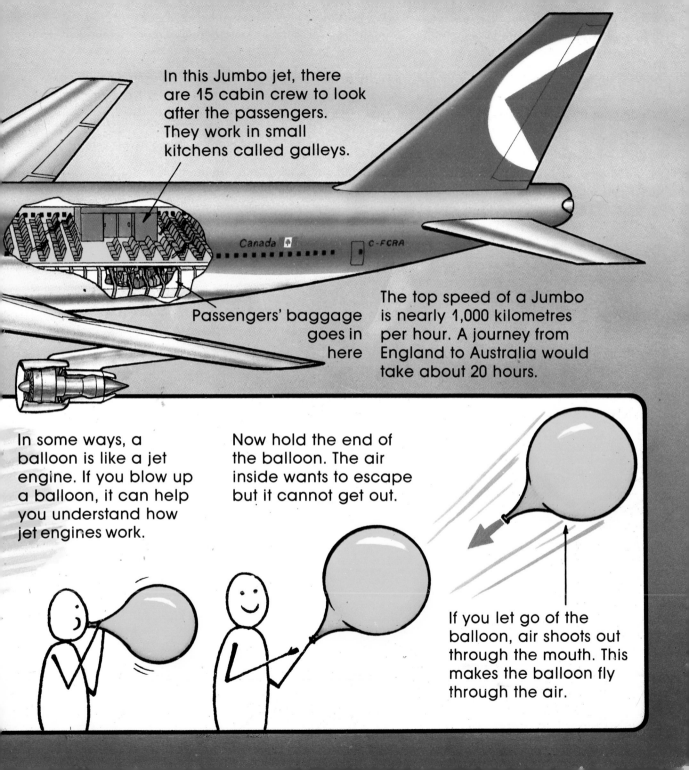

In this Jumbo jet, there are 15 cabin crew to look after the passengers. They work in small kitchens called galleys.

Canada ⚜ C-FCRA

Passengers' baggage goes in here

The top speed of a Jumbo is nearly 1,000 kilometres per hour. A journey from England to Australia would take about 20 hours.

In some ways, a balloon is like a jet engine. If you blow up a balloon, it can help you understand how jet engines work.

Now hold the end of the balloon. The air inside wants to escape but it cannot get out.

If you let go of the balloon, air shoots out through the mouth. This makes the balloon fly through the air.

Balloons

1 Hot air balloons are filled with hot air. This is lighter than the air outside, so the balloon floats. Three or four people can ride in a balloon. They usually do this just for fun.

2 The balloon is spread out on the ground. The mouth of the balloon is held open while the burner fills it with hot air.

3 The balloon is inflated by blowing hot air into the bag, using a gas burner. Hot air is lighter than the cold air, so the balloon lifts up.

4 To keep the balloon in the air, the air inside it is kept hot with short bursts of flame. Balloons cannot be steered easily. They go where the wind blows them.

5 There is a large metal bottle in each corner of the basket. These carry the gas which the burner burns.

6 The pilot uses the burner to control the height of the balloon. The hotter he makes the air inside, the higher the basket rises.

Across the ocean

In 1978 three Americans made the first successful crossing of the Atlantic Ocean in a balloon, called Double Eagle. The journey from the U.S.A. to France took six days.

Double Eagle was filled with a gas called helium, which is much lighter than air.

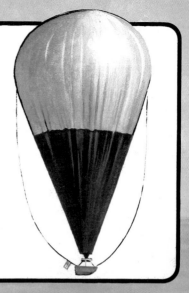

7 Steel wires join the basket to the balloon.

10 On the ground the pilot pulls a cord attached to a panel on the balloon. This opens up and the rest of the hot air in the balloon can escape.

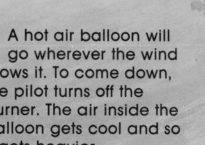

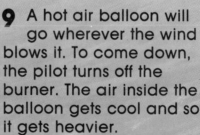

8 The balloon is made of nylon. The basket is made of willow branches woven together. This is strong and light.

9 A hot air balloon will go wherever the wind blows it. To come down, the pilot turns off the burner. The air inside the balloon gets cool and so it gets heavier.

1 Earlier rockets could only be used once. The Space Shuttle can be used many times. It takes scientific instruments up into space to study the stars and the planets.

Hot gas rushes out here

Liquid oxygen tank

Fuel and oxygen mix and burn in here

Fuel tank

Inside a rocket, fuel like petrol burns with oxygen to make very hot gases. The gases expand and rush out through the back. When this happens the rocket is pushed forward.

4 Space Shuttle can orbit the Earth for as long as 30 days without landing. It can fly 160 kilometres above the Earth.

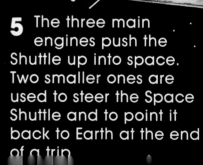

2 To help it take off, the Space Shuttle needs a big fuel tank and two extra rockets.

3 After eight minutes the rockets fall back to Earth. The fuel tank drops off when it is used up.

5 The three main engines push the Shuttle up into space. Two smaller ones are used to steer the Space Shuttle and to point it back to Earth at the end of a trip.

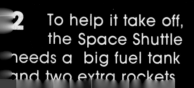

plane. The living area is under the flight control deck.

7 This is a solar panel. It takes in light from the Sun and turns it into electricity. Machines that the Shuttle carries can use the electricity.

Living quarters

USA

10 When the Space Shuttle comes back to Earth, it glows red hot from air friction.

8 The top of the Space Shuttle opens up. Then the scientific instruments can study the parts of

9 The part of the Space Shuttle that opens up can also be used to carry satellites into space. The satellite would leave the plane

11 The Space Shuttle lands just like an ordinary

Helicopters

Helicopters take off straight up into the air. They can fly forwards, backwards or sideways. They can also hover in one place.

The pictures below show you how the pilot can control a helicopter by tilting the blades.

The engine is at the top of a helicopter, in the middle. It makes a rod spin round very fast. This turns the blades round.

Fast air

Slower air

Helicopters like this can go as fast as 250 kilometres per hour.

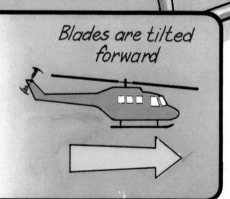

A helicopter blade is shaped like the wing of an aeroplane. It is curved on top and flat on the bottom.

1 Going up

The engine turns the blades round very fast. This lifts the helicopter into the air. The blades are level.

Blades are level so helicopter rises

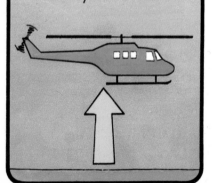

2 Going forward

When the pilot tilts the blades down at the front, the helicopter flies forward. The blades go round very fast. This pulls the helicopter along.

Blades are tilted forward

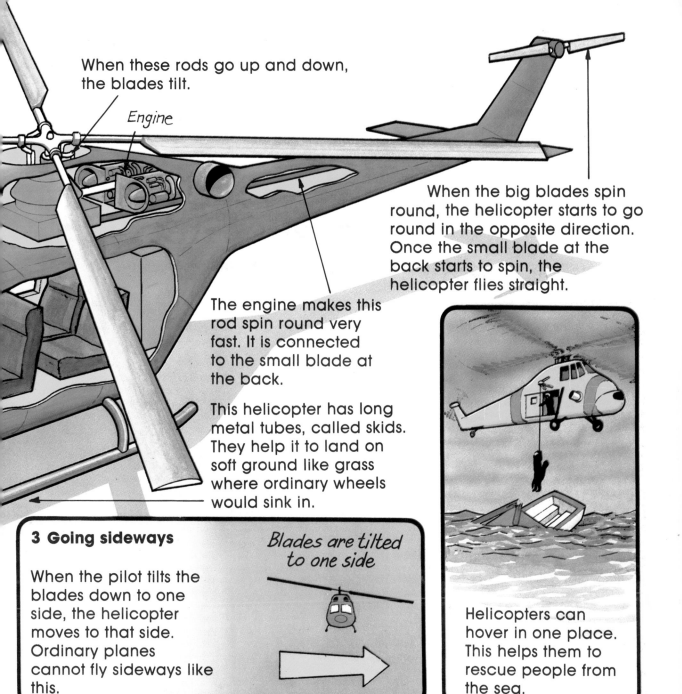

When these rods go up and down, the blades tilt.

Engine

When the big blades spin round, the helicopter starts to go round in the opposite direction. Once the small blade at the back starts to spin, the helicopter flies straight.

The engine makes this rod spin round very fast. It is connected to the small blade at the back.

This helicopter has long metal tubes, called skids. They help it to land on soft ground like grass where ordinary wheels would sink in.

3 Going sideways

When the pilot tilts the blades down to one side, the helicopter moves to that side. Ordinary planes cannot fly sideways like this.

Blades are tilted to one side

Helicopters can hover in one place. This helps them to rescue people from the sea.

Trains

Here are some of the different kinds of engines that can be used to pull trains.

Steam

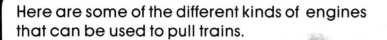

Early trains were pulled by steam engines. These burnt coal to make power. The train above is the American Empire State Express, No 999. In 1892 it went over 160 kilometres per hour.

Diesel

Small shunting locomotives, like the one above, are often run by diesel engines. They are used to move freight wagons about in goods yards.

Electric

Some electric trains take their electricity from overhead wires. This one is Japanese. It is called the Bullet Train. It can go over 250 kilometres per hour.

Inside a diesel electric locomotive

This is a modern British locomotive called an HST (which stands for 'High Speed Train').

It uses a diesel engine and a generator to make electricity for the electric motors. HSTs can go 200 kilometres per hour.

3 The motors

The wheels are turned by electric motors just above the axle. They run on the electricity from the generator.

1 The engine

The diesel engine is very powerful. It is stronger than a bus or lorry engine. It runs off diesel fuel, which is like petrol.

2 The generator

A rod that comes from the engine to the generator spins round very fast. Inside the generator, this spinning movement makes electricity.

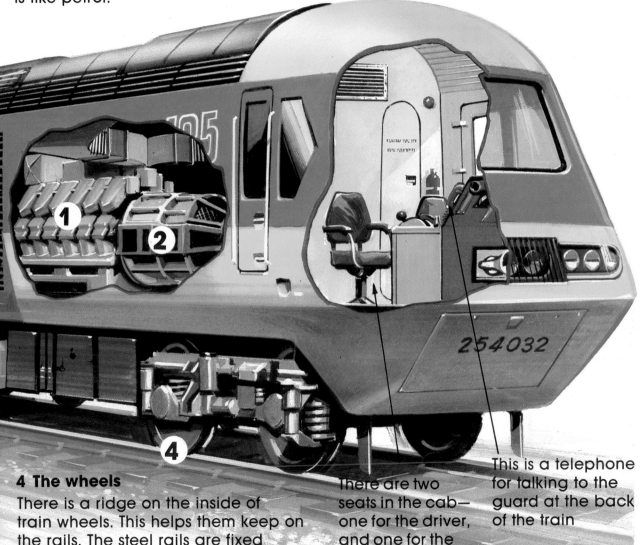

4 The wheels

There is a ridge on the inside of train wheels. This helps them keep on the rails. The steel rails are fixed to sleepers made of wood or concrete.

There are two seats in the cab— one for the driver, and one for the co-driver.

This is a telephone for talking to the guard at the back of the train

Bicycles

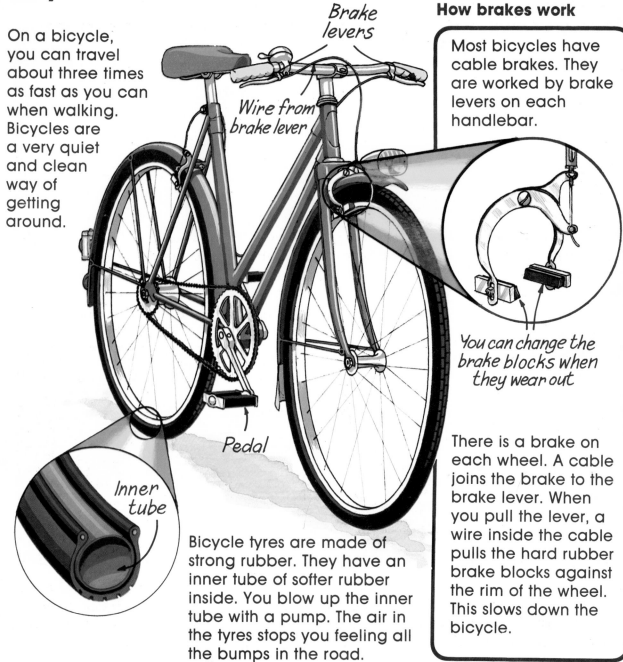

On a bicycle, you can travel about three times as fast as you can when walking. Bicycles are a very quiet and clean way of getting around.

Brake levers

Wire from brake lever

Pedal

Inner tube

Bicycle tyres are made of strong rubber. They have an inner tube of softer rubber inside. You blow up the inner tube with a pump. The air in the tyres stops you feeling all the bumps in the road.

How brakes work

Most bicycles have cable brakes. They are worked by brake levers on each handlebar.

You can change the brake blocks when they wear out

There is a brake on each wheel. A cable joins the brake to the brake lever. When you pull the lever, a wire inside the cable pulls the hard rubber brake blocks against the rim of the wheel. This slows down the bicycle.

How a bicycle moves

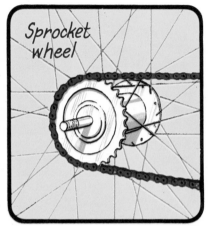

The pedals are fixed to a large chain wheel. When you push on the pedals the chain wheel goes round. The chain fits over the teeth of the chain wheel, so when the chain wheel is turned, the chain is pulled round.

At the back of the bicycle, the chain fits over a small sprocket wheel. This is joined to the back wheel.

The sprocket wheel goes round about three times every time you pedal the chain wheel round once. This is because the chain wheel has about three times as many teeth as the sprocket wheel.

The sprocket wheel turns the back wheel several turns for every one turn of the pedals.

23

Machines on a building site

There is a crane on the back of this lorry. It can lift heavy things like iron girders and pipes.

At the end of the crane, which is fixed to the lorry, there is a motor. This winds the steel cable and makes the hook go up and down.

Bulldozers scrape the ground level and shovel up earth. A bulldozer needs tracks made of steel links to help it go along rough ground. These are turned by a powerful diesel engine.

Steel tracks

How a bulldozer turns

Bulldozer tracks cannot turn like the front wheels of a lorry. If a bulldozer has to turn a corner, the driver makes the track on the outside of the curve go faster than the one on the inside. This pulls the bulldozer round.

This track goes fast

This track goes fast

These tracks go slower

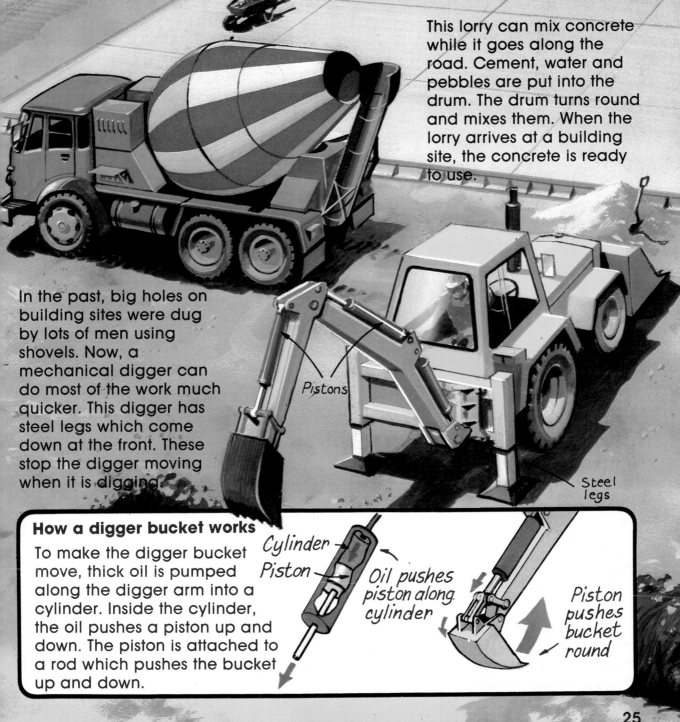

This lorry can mix concrete while it goes along the road. Cement, water and pebbles are put into the drum. The drum turns round and mixes them. When the lorry arrives at a building site, the concrete is ready to use.

In the past, big holes on building sites were dug by lots of men using shovels. Now, a mechanical digger can do most of the work much quicker. This digger has steel legs which come down at the front. These stop the digger moving when it is digging.

Pistons

Steel legs

How a digger bucket works

To make the digger bucket move, thick oil is pumped along the digger arm into a cylinder. Inside the cylinder, the oil pushes a piston up and down. The piston is attached to a rod which pushes the bucket up and down.

Cylinder

Piston

Oil pushes piston along cylinder

Piston pushes bucket round

25

The parts of a car

This picture shows you the important parts of a car. We have taken away part of the car body, so you can see inside.

In most cars the engine is in the front and it makes the car go by turning the back wheels.

The petrol tank

This is the tank which holds petrol for the engine.

The springs

When you go over bumps in the road, the springs stop the passengers feeling the bumps.

The tyres

Car tyres are made of thick rubber. The tyres are filled with air. They have patterns, called treads, cut into them to help the car grip the road.

The boot

The boot for carrying luggage is just above the petrol tank.

Petrol goes in here

The silencer

The engine makes a lot of dirty smoke and noise. These go along the exhaust pipe and through the silencer. The silencer takes away much of the noise.

The hand brake

This is the handbrake. It is used when the car is parked. When the car is moving, the driver uses the foot brake.

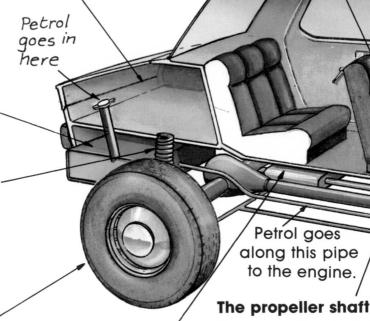

Petrol goes along this pipe to the engine.

Brake pipe

The propeller shaft

The propeller shaft is a long rod. It joins the engine to the back wheels and makes them go round.

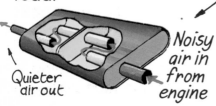

Quieter air out

Noisy air in from engine

Propeller shaft

Back axle

The windscreen

The windscreen is made of extra strong glass, so it will not break easily.

The battery

The battery provides electricity to help start the engine and work the lights.

The brakes

There is a brake on each wheel. The outside of the brake goes round with the wheel. Inside the brake there are two pads.

When you press on the brake pedal, a liquid in the brake pipes makes the pads press against the part of the brake that goes round.

Brake pipe

These pads press outwards

This part goes round with the wheel

Gearbox

The brake is in here

Brake pipe

The engine

The engine makes the wheels in the gearbox turn round and these make the propeller shaft spin. This makes the back axle spin and the back wheels go round. You can see how the engine works on the next page.

The accelerator

When you press down on the accelerator pedal, more petrol goes into the engine and the car goes faster.

The steering

To go round a corner, you turn the steering wheel to left or right. It is linked to a rod which turns the front wheels.

How a car engine works

Engine

Engine

Most cars have engines in the front, which make the back wheels go round.

Some cars have engines in the front, which make the front wheels go round.

Some cars have engines in the back, which make the back wheels go round.

A car cylinder cut in half

Inside a car engine there are four or more metal tubes called cylinders. When the engine is working, a piece of metal called a piston goes up and down inside each cylinder. The picture below shows a cylinder cut in half.

Petrol and air go in here

Spark plug

Exhaust gas comes out here

Petrol and air are sprayed into the top of the cylinder. A spark from the spark plug lights up the petrol and air, so they explode.

Piston

Connecting rod

When the petrol and air explode, they take up more space. This pushes the piston down the cylinder.

Crank-shaft

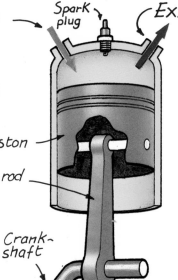

The connecting rod connects the piston to the crankshaft. It swings from side to side in the bottom of the piston as the piston goes up and down.

The connecting rod makes the crankshaft turn round.

The picture below shows a car engine with its side cut away so you can see how the pistons go up and down inside the cylinders. The pistons turn the crankshaft. The crankshaft turns the propeller shaft and this makes the back wheels go round.

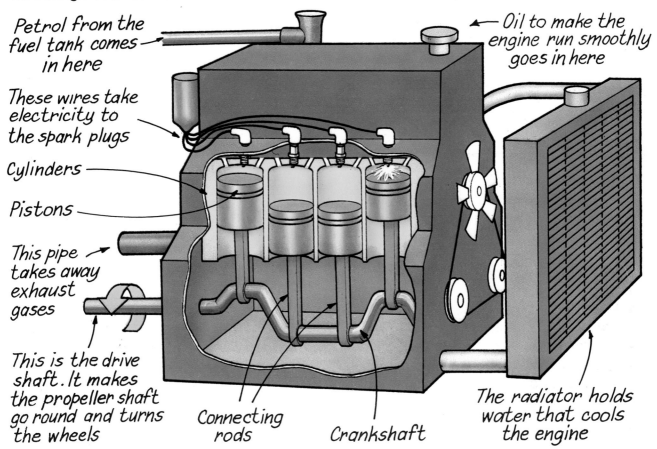

Petrol from the fuel tank comes in here

Oil to make the engine run smoothly goes in here

These wires take electricity to the spark plugs

Cylinders

Pistons

This pipe takes away exhaust gases

This is the drive shaft. It makes the propeller shaft go round and turns the wheels

Connecting rods

Crankshaft

The radiator holds water that cools the engine

When petrol and air explode in the top of the cylinders, they make the pistons go up and down. On the bottom of each piston is a connecting rod. This is joined to the crankshaft. When the pistons go up and down, they make the crankshaft turn the drive shaft round and round very fast.

The story of things that go

1

The earliest boat was made from a log. Later, several logs were tied together to make a raft.

2

5,000 years ago, the Egyptians made boats from reeds. These were used for carrying grain.

3

The wheel was invented over 4,000 years ago. It made it much easier to move heavy objects.

7

In 1820 the first bicycle was made from wood. It had no chain and was called a hobby horse.

8

The first plane to fly was a glider built in 1852. The passenger was a ten year old English boy.

9

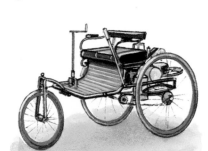

The first car driven by a petrol engine was made by Karl Benz in Germany in 1885.

4

The first submarine was made of wood. It was built by an American in 1775 and could only carry one man.

5

The first boat with an engine was made in France in 1783. Its steam engine worked two paddle wheels.

6

Early trains were steam trains. The first steam locomotive pulled a train in 1804.

10

In 1903 the first plane to fly with an engine was built by the Wright brothers in the U.S.A.

11

The first jet plane to fly was the Heinkel He 178. It was made in Germany in 1939.

12

The first rocket to carry a person into space was the Russian Vostok. It was launched in 1961.

Index

©1981 Usborne Publishing Ltd.

First published in 1981 by
Usborne Publishing Ltd, 20
Garrick Street, London
WC2E 9BJ

The type was set in
Avant Garde
by F. J. Milner & Sons Ltd,
Brentford, Middlesex

Printed in Belgium

The name Usborne and the device are
Trade Marks of Usborne Publishing Ltd.